THIS CANDLEWICK BOOK BELONGS TO:

For the Yoo-hoo Girls,
for all the times
we're stuck in the
muck together
P. R.

For Tim
J. C.

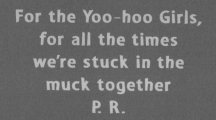

First U.S. paperback edition 2003

The Library of Congress has cataloged the hardcover edition as follows:

Root, Phyllis.
One duck stuck / Phyllis Root ;
illustrated by Jane Chapman.— 1st U.S. ed.
p.   cm.
Summary: In this counting book, increasingly larger groups of
animals try to help a duck that is stuck in the sleepy, slimy marsh.
ISBN 0-7636-0334-1 (hardcover)
[1. Ducks—Fiction. 2. Marsh animals—Fiction. 3. Counting.
4. Stories in rhyme.] I Chapman, Jane, date, –ill. II. Title.
PZ8.3.R667On 1998 [F]—dc21   97-34103

ISBN 0-7636-1566-8 (paperback)

4 6 8 10 9 7 5 3

Printed in China

This book was typeset in Myriad Tilt Bold.
The illustrations were done in gouache.

Candlewick Press
2067 Massachusetts Avenue
Cambridge, Massachusetts 02140

visit us at www.candlewick.com

One Duck Stuck

Phyllis Root illustrated by Jane Chapman

CANDLEWICK PRESS
CAMBRIDGE, MASSACHUSETTS

Down by the marsh,
by the sleepy,
slimy marsh,

1

one duck
gets stuck in the muck,
down by the
deep green marsh.

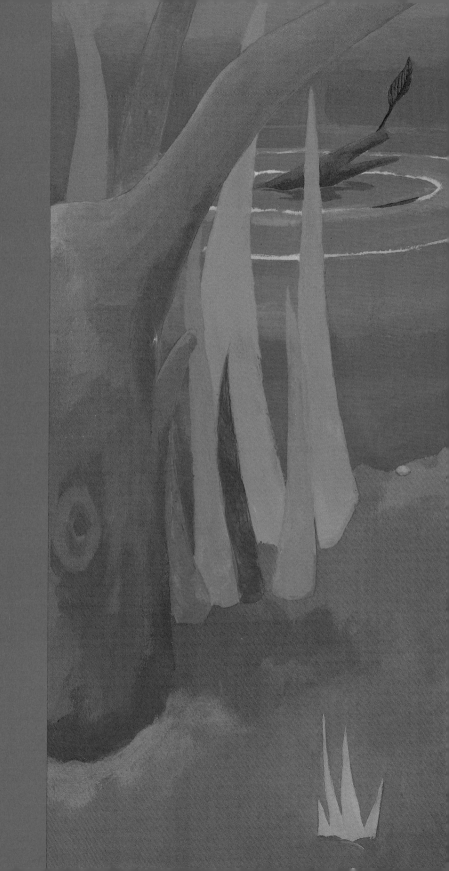

We can! We can!

2

Two fish,
tails going swish,
swim to the duck.

Splish, splish.

No luck.
The duck stays stuck
deep in the muck
down by the
squishy, fishy marsh.

We can! We can!

3

Three moose
munching on spruce
plod to the duck.

Clomp, clomp.

No luck.
The duck stays stuck
deep in the muck
down by the
swampy, chompy marsh.

We can! We can!

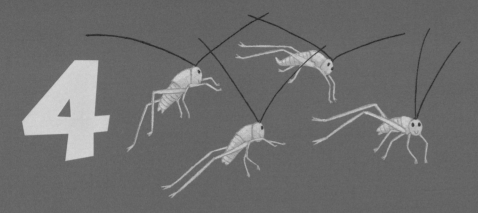

4

Four crickets
chirping in the thickets
leap to the duck.

Pleep, pleep.

No luck.
The duck stays stuck
deep in the muck
down by the
pricky, sticky marsh.

We can! We can!

5

Five frogs
hopping on logs
jump to the duck.

Plop, plop.

No luck.
The duck stays stuck
deep in the muck
down by the
creaky, croaky marsh.

Help!
Help!

Who
can
help?

We can! We can!

6

Six skunks
climbing over trunks
crawl to the duck.

Plunk, plunk.

No luck.
The duck stays stuck
deep in the muck
down by the
soggy, loggy marsh.

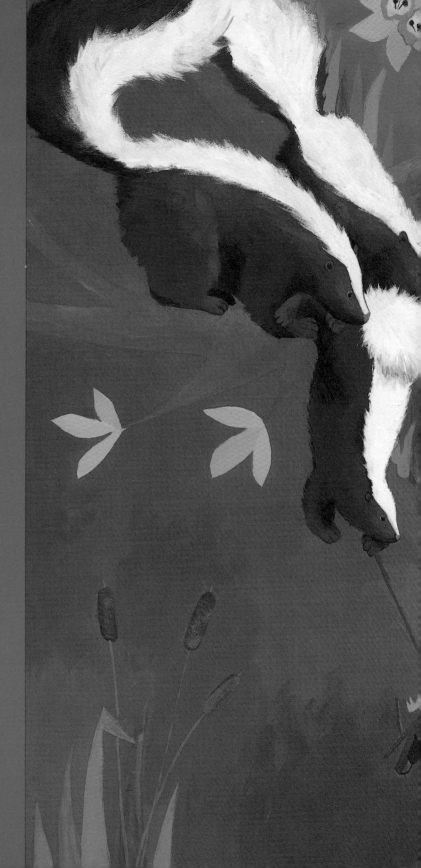

Help!
Help!

Who
can
help?

We can! We can!

7

Seven snails
making slippery trails
slide to the duck.

Sloosh, sloosh.

No luck.
The duck stays stuck
deep in the muck
down by the
slippy, sloppy marsh.

We can! We can!

8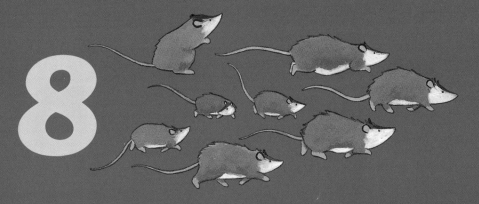

Eight possums
nibbling on blossoms
crawl to the duck.

Slosh, slosh.

No luck.
The duck stays stuck
deep in the muck
down by the
reedy, weedy marsh.

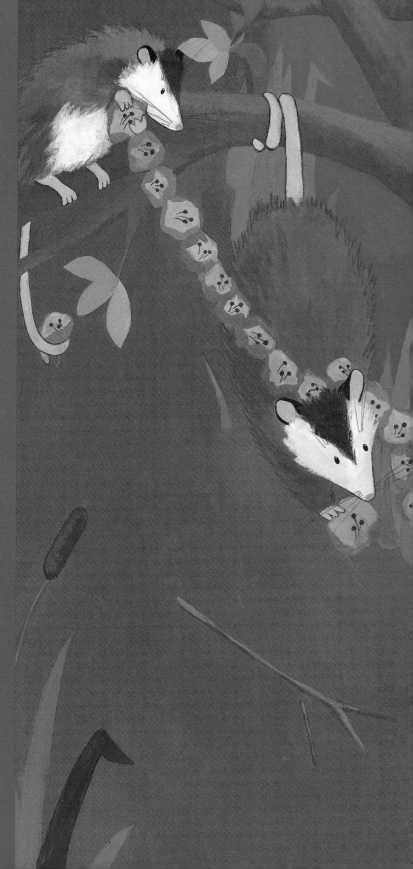

Help!
Help!

Who
can
help?

We can! We can!

9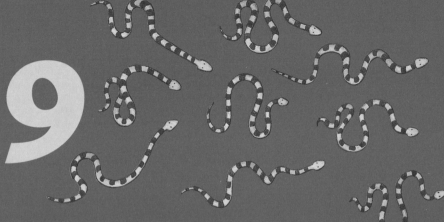

Nine snakes
leaving little wakes
slither to the duck.

Slink, slink.

No luck.
The duck stays stuck
deep in the muck
down by the
messy, mossy marsh.

We can! We can!

10

Ten dragonflies
zooming through the skies
whir to the duck.

Zing, zing.

No luck.
The duck stays stuck
deep in the muck
down by the
muggy, buggy marsh.

Help!
Help!

Who
can
help?

We can!

We can!

splish

clomp

pleep

plop

plunk

sloosh

slosh

slink

zing

They **all** help the duck who got stuck in the muck.

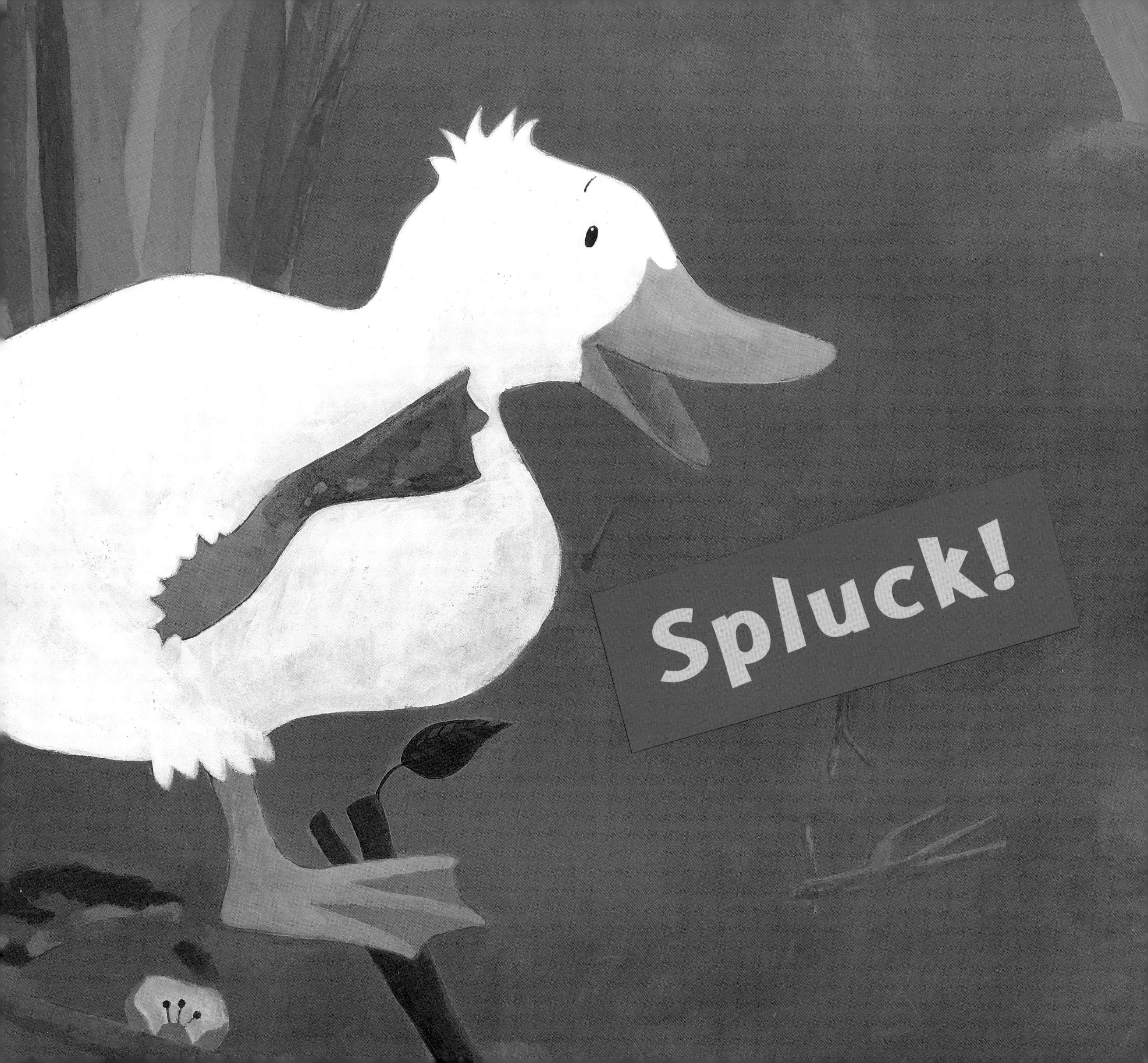
Spluck!

"Thanks!"
said the duck
who got out
of the muck

down

by the

deep

green

marsh.

PHYLLIS ROOT has written many children's books, including *Oliver Finds His Way*, illustrated by Christopher Denise; *Big Momma Makes the World*, illustrated by Helen Oxenbury; *Rattletrap Car* and *What Baby Wants*, both illustrated by Jill Barton; and *Kiss the Cow!*, illustrated by Will Hillenbrand. She says she wanted *One Duck Stuck* to be "a north woods wetlands counting book, accurate to the marshes of Minnesota. All the animals are actually found there. I love to go canoeing and camping, and this book is a composite of my experiences." Phyllis Root lives in Minnesota.

JANE CHAPMAN does all her painting in her kitchen, looking out onto the garden. "The color blue in *One Duck Stuck* is the exact same blue that's in my kitchen," she says. Although she has a pet tortoise named Muggs, who at over seventy years old is a family heirloom, one day she would like to have a duck as well. Jane Chapman is the illustrator of *The Emperor's Egg* by Martin Jenkins, *One Tiny Turtle* by Nicola Davies, and *The Story of Christmas* by Vivian French.